The
YOUNGEST
CAMEL

The

YOUNGEST
CAMEL

Reconsidered and Rewritten
by KAY BOYLE

Pictures by Ronni Solbert

HARPER & BROTHERS
Publishers NEW YORK

FOR
Sindbad, Pegeen, Bobby, Apple,
Kathe, Clover, Faith, and *Ian*
and *their children*

I

The caravan set off through lovely country, moving between fields and marshes where tea-roses and white and purple iris bloomed. When it passed through villages, boys ran out, barefoot and half-naked, to sell baskets of peaches, pears, and melons to the travelers. All forty camels of the caravan had several little silver-tongued bells attached to the harnesses around their necks, and the sound of these bells was like music as they walked. The youngest camel was the only one who did not wear bells or carry a load. This was his first trip across the desert and he followed closely behind his mother. As long as she was there before him, he was not afraid of the new things he saw.

But after several days the caravan entered the badlands. Here the older camels became nervous and flew into sudden rages if anyone came near them. When the camel drivers jerked their nose cords and shouted at them, they flung their legs about and tottered as if they were about to faint. Even the youngest camel did not like the queer shapes of the rocks and the steepness of the paths they had to follow. But as soon as the desert began, the camels stopped screaming and spitting, and walked quietly again, with the hot sand slipping away under their feet.

As the days passed, the youngest camel became more and more pleased with life. He came skipping and jumping along behind his mother, playing games with himself, and telling himself that he could never possibly get tired. But when his mother complained about the heat, and the

long way they still had to go, he lifted his soft dark eyes and looked at her bony legs before him, and he thought: I love her. I love her elbows with the hair worn off them, like the old carpet the snake charmer sits on in the market place. I love the way her hump slumps when she has no more water in it, and the way her poor thin tail hangs down.

He was a poetic young camel, and rather musical besides. He had a fine singing voice, and in the evenings when they halted to rest at an oasis he liked to sing to his mother. Most of his songs were about himself, but

sometimes at night his songs were so tender in his love for her that she had to rise from her knees and wipe the tears from her face with the great leaves of the banana trees.

On the fifteenth night they halted at an oasis where mimosa bushes made yellow velvet tents for them and where hares and antelope moved shyly through the cool green gorges. The youngest camel lay close beside his mother in the moist grasses, and he watched the stars that were sprinkled out as fine as salt across the blue night sky.

"Blossom of my heart, this trip you have followed at my heels, for you are my baby still," his mother said to him; "but soon you must prepare yourself for what will surely come. Perhaps when we reach the end of this journey you will be taken from me, and from then on you will travel with strange camels, carrying a load of your own."

"A baby?" said the youngest camel in surprise. "I'm not a baby!"

"Well, anyway, you are my earliest leaf," said his mother, and her voice was very sad to hear. "Very soon now you will have to undergo the ordeal of loneliness."

"What in the world is that?" asked the youngest camel.

"The ordeal of loneliness is the thing that camels fear the most in life," said his mother, and he sat listening rather impatiently to her, swinging his little golden chin back and forth as he chewed on a bit of grass. "Men have found out that what we fear more than anything else is being left alone. So they take us when we are very young, like you, and they tie us fast and leave us in solitude for three days and three nights in the desert. If we live through that, then we are no longer afraid of the sight of loneliness all around us. But sometimes we become so frightened that we do not live through it. You must be prepared for that."

"Why, I wouldn't mind being alone at all!" said the youngest camel with a laugh. "I'm a little bit afraid of fire, and I don't like things that lie still and don't move any more, but generally I'm much more brave than other young camels. I couldn't possibly be afraid of being alone!"

Danger seemed a thing too far away to think of, even, for all around them the oasis was filled with sleeping life. The mules of the caravan were tethered under the poplar trees, and their tails swung lazily back and forth in the warm night air. Against the starry sky, the heads and the tall necks of the kneeling camels stood as motionless as statues.

"At first you will be very much afraid," his mother went on, "but you must try to remember there is nothing really to fear. It is sometimes only the beating of our own hearts that makes us tremble."

"That's silly," said the youngest camel, and he nibbled at a mimosa leaf.

"Perhaps the time has now come for me to tell you of one trick men use to separate baby camels from their mothers," she said, her voice as soft as the passing breeze. "They want the mother to join the caravan again, and so the little camel must give up drinking milk, and learn to eat. The camel drivers shave the mother clean and smooth, and her child does not recognize her because she hasn't any hair. He runs all through the village and fields looking for her, and when he sees a camel with hair, he runs quickly to it, and the strange camel puts back its ears and spits at him, and snaps its teeth. After a few days of this, he believes his mother has turned against him, and he is so hungry he can hardly stand, and so he begins to eat as the older camels do."

"But I'd always know you. They couldn't possibly fool me," said the youngest camel with great assurance. And then he saw the tears on her face taking the light of the stars. "Don't cry about me, please," he said, and his voice grew more gentle.

"I'm not crying over you, my cactus flower, but because of the cruelty of men," his mother said.

12

II

The youngest camel awoke the next day at dawn, and he felt as gay as a lark. He sang so loudly as he splashed in the waters of the oasis pool that the mules craned their heads over their shoulders and looked severely at him. Then he caught sight of a group of melancholy wading birds breakfasting on frogs, and he crept up behind them through the reeds, and jumped out at them, scaring them so that they spread their wings and flew away.

His mother was not feeling as sentimental as she had the night before, for the sun was rising beyond the tamarisk trees and a day's travel lay before them. All the time she was being saddled and packed, she kept darting black looks at her son who was dancing foolishly around, but she couldn't get near enough to him to say a word. And then when the caravan started off again across the sand, the youngest camel did not keep behind his mother as he had on the other days. He ran lightly along beside her, humming to the music of the camels' silver bells, and ready to lead the caravan if they asked him to.

"The trouble with children is that they can't see things as they really are," his mother said to him under her breath, and she stretched out her neck and tried to nip his ear.

"Well, how are things really?" the youngest camel asked, skipping quickly out of reach.

"Things are exactly as they are," snapped his mother as she ambled along behind the next camel's hind legs and tail. The sun was rising higher above them, and every instant it grew hotter, until, as the hours passed, the heat seemed to have bleached all the color out of the sky. "The sand is as hot as burning coals," his mother went on, "and there is no stopping place until we reach the oasis, which will be about sundown. Such things *are*. Also, there is a sore on my right hip that is being rubbed at every step by the leather of my haunch strap. Whether you like them or not, these things exist."

"What about the things that aren't?" asked the youngest camel, and he gave a leap after a sand flea that went jumping past.

"One of the things that isn't is the green vale I had always hoped to settle in when I got old," said his mother. "At my time of life, I ought to have a place like that where I could stretch out and eat all the fresh leaves I wanted and drink as much cool water as I—" The camel driver gave her mouth such a jerk at that moment that she had to stop speaking for a moment, and after a little while she added bitterly: "Those are some of the things that can never possibly be."

"What about the caravan of white camels with solid gold hoofs that goes right around the earth like a belt?" asked the youngest camel.

"It doesn't exist," said his mother shortly.

"But a llama told me that back in Sandistan," the little camel said. "The white camels go right around the world through everything—through cities, and oceans, and palaces, and over mountains. They keep on going all the time and nothing can stop them and nobody except camels can see them. And whenever a camel is lost any-where in the world he only has to join the caravan of snow-white camels with gold hoofs, and in the end he's bound to pass through his own country, and find his mother again—"

"You can be sure that is one of the things that decid-edly is *not*," said his mother emphatically. Her feet were beginning to hurt her very much.

They went on in silence for a while, and then the little camel began asking questions again.

"What about the two sides of the weather that Moham-med has for a fan?" he said. "The light blue side is turned toward him when he feels like dancing and singing, and then the dark side of the fan is turned to us. And when he is deep in thought, he fans himself with the dark side so he won't be disturbed by the light. That's how we have good weather sometimes, and other times it's bad."

"That's what's known as a myth," said his mother. "Sometimes the sun shines and sometimes the rain falls. That's all there is to the weather story."

"What about the sun being a pineapple with the skin taken off?" said the youngest camel a little sadly.

"Impossible," said his mother.

"The peacock I met in Berbela said bad weather came whenever the wind blew hard and blew the biggest pine-apple from the tree and split it in a thousand pieces," the little camel said.

His mother gave a snort, and before she could say more, the little camel cried out:

"Oh, I've found the most wonderful thing you've ever seen! Oh, it's so marvelous! I found it—lying—right— here—in—the—sand—"

Because his voice grew fainter and fainter, she knew he must have stopped behind her to pick up whatever it was, but when she tried walking slower to give him time to catch up with her again, the camel driver pulled fiercely at her rein. She could not so much as turn her head to see what had become of her son, but she had to go loping on with the queer, sad smile on her lips which camels usually wear.

They had not gone very far before she heard her child panting behind her, and in another moment he called out:

"This time I've found a fortune! We're going to be rich and happy forever and you'll never have to work again! It's a string of wonderful beads." He was still out of breath. "Some of them are carved, and they're all different colors, and they're strung together on a solid silver chain. It must have been a prince or a rajah who lost them on his way to his wedding," his excited voice went on.

"They must be the most valuable string of beads in the whole world!"

The sun was growing hotter and hotter in the heavens, and his mother couldn't crane her neck around to see what the youngest camel was doing, and her feet hurt her, and her hip was rubbed quite raw.

"You'll have to turn the necklace over to the police as soon as we reach civilization," she said to him in annoyance. "It doesn't belong to you."

"Oh, but look!" the little camel cried out as if it were possible for her to turn her head and see. "There's a card tied to them, and something is written on it. It says—let me see a minute." He stopped talking now, and she knew he must be trying to make the letters out. "It says," he went on presently, " 'Whoever finds these magic beads may keep them.' So you see!" he cried out in the greatest joy. "Now they belong to us, and we can sell them in the next city, and you can have everything you want to make you happy. You can have a parasol to keep the sun off you, and a litter with curtains at both sides to be carried in by slaves, and you can wear a solid gold ring in your nose every day, and I can have a big mirror to watch myself in while I'm dancing, and—"

"Tell me what they look like," said his mother, beginning to be very curious. "This brute is holding the cord so tight I can't look around, but describe them to me."

"Well, one is bright red," said her son, following quickly behind her. "The next one is green, and the next after that shines like a diamond." He talked very slowly, as if he were examining the necklace as he came along at her heels. "And now I see something else!" he cried out in excitement. "Each one of the beads has a sort of message written in it, carved inside it in beautiful, tiny lettering."

"Ho, ho," said his mother. "That's probably why they're called magic beads."

"Oh, yes, I hadn't thought of that," said the youngest camel in a very innocent-sounding voice. "The jade one has written inside it," he went on slowly, as if he was having difficulty making out the words: " 'I am the green vale you long for. You may live in me forever.' And the topaz bead says: 'I am a silk tent to protect you from sandstorms and from rain and from the midday sun.' And the ruby one says: 'I am blood to flow in your veins and the veins of those you love. Thus you may live forever.' And the—"

"Do any of the beads say anything about shells?" asked

his mother suddenly, and the little camel looked up in surprise.

"Shells?" he repeated.

"Yes, sea-shells," said his mother. "Perhaps I haven't told you about sea-shells yet, but if you don't know, it's certainly time you did. Sea-shells are the best things in the world to eat, and they're very good for the teeth and hoofs."

"Oh, yes," said the little camel, as if he had been searching all this time for it and had just found it in the string. "Here is a bead as white as ivory, and all around it there is something written in gold. Yes, shells," he murmured. "I think it does say something about shells."

"Read it quickly!" his mother cried out, and after a moment or two of hesitation the youngest camel began reading aloud very slowly and uncertainly:

"If it's shells from the sea
That you crave, attach me
To your ankle. With what a commotion
Oysters, clams, periwinkles will rise
  from the ocean,
All shiny and brittle and richly embellished,
To be crunched, and then munched, and quite
  happily relished."

"Well, that's really wonderful," said his mother, and now she had forgotten about the heat, and how sore her hip was, and how long a way they had still to go. "I'm half tempted to have you try it out now, only it might be difficult if all the shells began to come right across the desert after us!"

"Oh, I don't think we ought to try it now!" said the youngest camel in some concern. "I think it would be much better if we waited until this evening when we've stopped to rest."

"Yes, I suppose you're right," said his mother. "But I can scarcely wait to try. Now tell me what's written inside the diamond. That sounds like the most beautiful one of all."

"Oh, the diamond," said her son slowly and thoughtfully, as if he were having a good look for it among the other beads. "Well, it's rather difficult to make out."

"I should think it would be very easy," said the mother camel. "It must be as clear as water, if it's a real diamond. I should think you could see what's written in it without any trouble at all."

"Well, the diamond takes the rays of the sun on every one of its points," said the little camel, "and so it practically blinds me, it dazzles so. But I think I can see something about 'drink' or 'water' written in it. Oh, yes," he went on after a moment, during which time his mother concluded he had been studying the jewel. "Oh, yes, now I can see! I've got it in the shadow of your tail and I can make out the words quite well. It says—let me see—yes, it says:

> 'When you would drink
> Just cease to think
> And bend your knee at my brink.'"

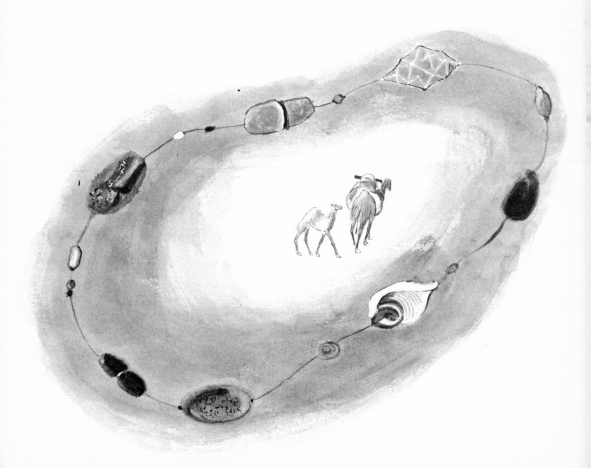

"Wonderful!" exclaimed his mother, and he could see by the way she ran youthfully over the sand that she had completely forgotten all her troubles and discomforts. So through the entire blazing hot day as they crossed the desert, he told her one by one the endless colors and verses of the beads. The amethyst was the jewel of memory, he told her, and you only had to hold it for a minute in your ear for all the nice things that had happened in the past to become the present. The moonstone was the bead of the future, and after you had rubbed it hard you could see reflected in it all that was going to happen. The sapphire was the bead of purity, and when you were old you need only press it for an instant against your forehead and all your years would drop from you like the petals from a flower.

"Ah, there's the oasis at last!" his mother cried out. The little camel lowered his head and peered through her legs, and there on the horizon, which had not altered during the entire day, he saw the distant dark points which must be the oasis trees. "The time passed very quickly, although I was so impatient to see the necklace every minute," his mother said. "But now in no time at all we can settle down and undo our packs and try the magic beads. The first one I'm going to try is the sapphire, so I need not be old any longer, and then the amethyst, so that all the nice things that happened to me before will come true again, and your father will be alive with us, and then—"

Strangely enough, the little camel now became silent. He said nothing at all, but simply followed in her footsteps, and once they had reached the green island in the vast white sea of sand, the mother camel turned eagerly to her son.

"Quickly now, come behind the trees and show me the necklace," she said in a whisper so that none of the other camels would hear, and she hurried him out of sight. But now that they were quite alone, the youngest camel only hung his head. "Quickly, quickly, where is it? I've never been so anxious to see anything in all my life—"

"Mother," said her child miserably. "There is no necklace."

"What? There is no necklace?" she cried, tottering back under the tamarisk trees. "Do you mean to say— oh, can it be possible—oh, good heavens, it can't be all a lie?"

"I don't know if it's a lie or not," said the little camel, and he turned unhappily away from the sight of her grief. "I made it up so you would forget about the heat, so perhaps it isn't as bad as lying. I kept thinking perhaps the necklace was really there, although I couldn't see it, like the caravan of white camels that girdles the earth, and like Mohammed—"

"Oh, this is too much!" moaned his mother, and her head hung low on her neck, and she swung it back and forth like a tolling bell. "I would never have dreamed —I never would have thought you could—I never, never—"

"But music's invisible, isn't it?" said the little camel in a gentle voice. "I kept on saying things like that to myself to make the necklace seem all right. I kept saying, 'Music's invisible and history's invisible and love's invisible and still they're all really there.'"

His mother had now sunk down on her knees onto the ground, and her son moved close to her and rubbed his soft nose in her neck.

"I wasn't sure you'd feel like singing me to sleep to-night," he said in a low voice. "After all that happened today, I thought you might rather not. So I made up the words of a lullaby, and if you're feeling too badly, I'll sing it to you instead."

His mother was weeping now, and she did not answer, and the youngest camel stood beside her in the tall grasses and he began to sing in a sad, beautiful voice through the night:

> *"Hush, sweet camel, drowsily dream,*
> *For only llamas spit and scream.*
> *If our coats are sand-colored*
>   *while theirs are cream,*
> *Remember, sweet mother, the dream*
>   *that we dream.*
> *In our humps we carry a treasure of jewels*
> *That we drink from the water of oasis pools,*
> *Jewel-box of the desert, my sand-queen,*
>   *my mother,*
> *Let us make our dreams true*
>   *with our love for each other."*

No sooner had he finished his song than two camel drivers came to where the youngest camel and his mother kneeled under the trees, and without speaking a word one of them put a rope around the little camel's neck. He was so surprised that he could not move, but his mother understood at once what was taking place, and she raised herself quickly from her knees and said to him in a soft voice:

"Do not resist them. Go quietly."

As they led him away, she hurried after him, calling:

"Be brave, my son. Think of me and remember all I have told you."

Then one of the men turned and raised his whip and struck her sharply on the soft part of the nose. She jumped back with a cry of pain, but long after they had started out across the dark desert, the little camel could hear her voice calling and calling to him.

"Go quietly! Do not struggle!" she cried. "Do not forget me! Perhaps one day we shall find each other again!"

III

The two men led the youngest camel far, far out into the desert, and after a long time, when they seemed to be out of sight and hearing of any living thing, they gave him the command to lie down. He had been brought up to look on man as master, and he kneeled obediently before them. Then they unwound the ropes from around their waists and pushed him over on his side. They drew his hind legs roughly forward and knotted them tightly to his forelegs and he never dreamed of kicking or protesting. He lay there very meekly on one side and allowed them to pass the ropes around his body and he did not make a sound. When their work was done, the camel drivers each gave him a parting kick and then went off in the direction from which they had come. He raised his head with difficulty from the sand, and he could see them moving away through the starlit night. But after a moment the two shapes muffled in their flowing robes were lost in the darkness, and the little camel realized he was alone, and he uttered one sudden terrible scream.

Now he knew beyond any doubt that this was the ordeal of loneliness, and he could not control the sobs that shook his body. All about him lay the warm, dark, desert silence, and there was no smell anywhere of camel or of man. He strained his ears until he thought they would fall from his head, but there was no sound of bells and not the faintest echo of his mother's voice calling to him. Everything was quiet as the tomb.

After some time had passed, he began kicking with all his strength. This was not such an easy matter because his feet were very firmly tied. But he doubled up his legs as best he could, and then shot them savagely out. But this only seemed to draw the cords tighter and tighter around his neck and shoulders, and it certainly made the knots cut deeper into his ankle bones. So presently he gave that up and tried lifting himself by pushing one shoulder and one hip hard against the ground. But now he got sand into both his eyes, and into his mouth. In his misery, he tried to remember all the things his mother had told him as they lay under the oasis trees at night. Once she had said to him:

34

"If a camel falls ill or is weakened by old age while crossing the desert, the men unsaddle and unload him and divide his pack among the others, and he is left alone there to die. His friends are forced on, screaming aloud with terror and despair and trying to look back over their shoulders at him as they go."

"If the truth is as terrible as all that," he had said to his mother, "I don't see why anyone pays any attention to it. I think it would be much better to make up something else instead."

And another night his mother had said to him:

"If we camels have silence in our ears, that is another thing that drives us out of our minds with fright. Perhaps that is the reason they hang bells around our necks, or perhaps that is why you like to sing so loudly at night when everything is still."

Remembering her words, the little camel began to sing in a high, quavering voice. He was in such a state of nerves that he didn't know what words he was singing, and the tune kept changing without him having anything to do with it, and he couldn't keep on the right key. But still he went on making up songs about nothing lasting forever, and about the swiftness of time flying by.

"All the time I am singing," he warbled in a high,

quavering voice, "time is passing, passing. The ordeal of loneliness will be over before I know it. The camel drivers will come back and fetch me, and I'll run as fast as I can after the caravan, and I'll find my mother—"

But when he reached the word "mother" his voice rose to a high wail and the tears rushed into his eyes and down his cheeks. Very soon after this, he must have cried himself to sleep, for when he awoke the sun was already rising. He rolled his eyes around in bewilderment a moment, and then he felt the ropes fast on his legs and neck, and the sand gritting between his teeth, and he knew where he was and why he was there. The sun rose and beat down hotter and hotter on him, and the sky seemed to be on fire above him, and it is quite probable that he became delirious as noon approached.

At one moment he thought he heard the faraway tinkling of camel bells, and he tried to call out, but he could not. A little later he thought he saw pomegranate flowers and fruit hanging on cool leafy branches before his eyes. He lay there gasping under the sun, and at times he believed that icy pools of water were just within reach, and at other times he thought that fresh ripe figs were just about to melt on his parched tongue. His eyes were glazed with fever now, and his mind was filled with

visions of strange and beautiful things. With his dry black lips he kept repeating:

"Music's invisible, history's invisible, love's invisible," and in the same faint voice he whispered at last: "Even hope's invisible, but it must be there just the same—"

As he uttered these words, he heard a gentle sigh like a breeze stirring the air, and the next instant a hand was laid on his forehead. He looked up through the thick waves of heat, and he saw a man standing beside him who now leaned over to stroke him, but strangely enough he could find no smell of man in his nostrils no matter how hard he sniffed.

"This must be a vision, too," he said to himself, but

at once the man began speaking to him in a sweet musical voice.

"I've been waiting for seventeen hours for you to say the magic word," said the man, and for some inexplicable reason he spoke a language which the youngest camel understood at once.

"What word?" the little camel whispered, and the man crossed his legs and sat down beside him on the sand. Then he raised the little camel's head and laid it on his silk-clad knees, and stroked back his hair as a mother might have done.

"I've been waiting for you to say 'hope,' " he answered. "As soon as you said that, it meant you hadn't given up, and then I was able to become visible and rescue you."

"Who are you?" asked the little camel in a low voice. He was almost too weak to keep his eyes open now, but he felt the man loosening the ropes that bound him, and this gave him the strength to speak.

"Oh, I'm one of Mohammed's sons," the man said. "I'm one of the youngest and unimportant ones. This year I've been given all the young camels in the world to keep an eye on. My father, whom you have doubtless bent the knee to as the great Prophet of Islam, is very wise, but still his heart has remained as gentle as the play-

ing of flutes. Long ago, when he was young and still mortal, he led caravans across the desert like an ordinary man, and so he knows what camel children suffer. That's why he sent me here." While he talked, he kept undoing the ropes and drawing them from under the little camel's hot body, and shaking them free of his ankles, where they had cut deep into the flesh. "If you had mentioned the word 'hope' sooner instead of talking about 'music' and 'history' and 'love' I could have freed you hours and hours ago. 'Hope' is a magic word in any language, and it permits me to become human for a little while and help young camels who have been bound up by men."

"What makes hope magic?" asked the youngest camel, and he stretched out one stiff leg to see if he could still move it. And now Mohammed's son lifted him higher against his shoulder and shook the remaining cords away. When he did this, the little camel saw that Mohammed's son was young and very handsome. On his head he wore a silk turban with pearls and turquoises embroidered on it, and carved gold ornaments hung from his ears, and there was a look of great gentleness in his face.

"Well, you see, 'h' stands for 'help,' and 'o' stands for 'O,' and 'p' stands for 'power,' and 'e' stands for 'eternal,' " he said, speaking lightly and merrily. He took a little flask

from the folds of his silken garments and poured some fresh water between the little camel's burning lips. "So when you say 'hope' like that, you're really saying 'Help, O power eternal!' And I'm your power eternal this year because I've been appointed to watch over you. I'm sorry I can't give you anything to eat," Mohammed's son went on as he patted the little camel's cheek, "but it's really too difficult to travel around invisible with a lot of mimosa branches and sea-shells and things like that hanging on me. But if you're feeling strong enough now, I can start you off in the direction of Asquzand."

"Oh, please, don't leave me alone! Please stay with me until I find the caravan again!" the youngest camel pleaded. But Mohammed's son shook his head gently and smiled.

"You see, there are lots of other young camels in the same situation you were in when I came along, and I have to rescue them too, if it's not too late," he said. "But most of them just won't use the word 'hope,' so I usually have to leave them there bound up. I think it's a little stupid of them not to perceive that hope is one of the few things to call on when they're in trouble, but there's nothing I can do." The youngest camel was feeling so much better by this time that he was able to stand up and look around him. He thought to himself that certainly no one had ever had any reason to call him stupid, and he began to feel rather pleased with all the exceptional things he was. "No matter what happens to you now, I won't be able to help you any further," said Mohammed's son. "My father made a rule that the guardian of the young camels could give help only to those whom men had bound up in the desert. So I must be on my way."

By this time the youngest camel was quite certain that nothing further could possibly happen to him, and he even managed to shake himself with pleasure as Mohammed's son shaded his eyes with his hand and looked up at the blazing sky.

"You must follow in the direction of the sun," the young man said. "If you do that, you will be in Asquzand just as night is beginning to fall. Remember not to let the sun show either over your right shoulder or over your left. That will mean you are going in the wrong direction. Just sixty caravan-lengths from Asquzand, you will come to an oasis with hundreds of herons wading in the waters and flamingos flying through the trees. When you reach that oasis, you will know for certain that you haven't much farther to go. If you do as I say, you can't possibly make a mistake."

The little camel began to wonder if he had ever in his entire life made a mistake, and he couldn't think of a single time he had. Perhaps the thought that was in his mind showed in his face, for Mohammed's son smiled patiently at him again and put one arm around his neck. He said:

"You know, there is one thing in life that is very important, and that is to be humble."

"Is it?" said the youngest camel, and from the smile on his mouth it was quite clear that he didn't believe it for a moment. It's very important to be clever and funny and brave, he thought, and I'm all those things most of the time, but where in the world would humility get you in the end? Because he did not feel at all humble, he said out loud: "Would it be possible for you to let my mother know that I'm—"

"No," said Mohammed's son, and a look of sorrow came like a cloud across his face. "I couldn't do that. Little camel, do not think so much about yourself. Remember, the desert is a blank piece of paper on which you write the story of what you are."

"I don't think that's a very good idea," said the youngest camel, "because the wind could come along and blow the whole story away."

As he spoke these words, Mohammed's son looked sadly at him from his great, dark eyes, and then vanished as suddenly as he had appeared. Without wasting another instant, the little camel turned his head toward the sun and began to run as fast as he could in the direction of Asquzand.

IV

At four o'clock in the afternoon the little camel was still running hard. By now it seemed to him that some sort of object was taking shape on the horizon, far, far away. Whatever it was, it was not ahead of him as Mohammed's son had told him the oasis would be, and he kept glancing out of the corner of his eye at it. Then he began to run a little slower, for the thought came to him that perhaps Mohammed's son had been mistaken. After a while he stopped running entirely, and turned halfway around, and gave the dark object a good long stare. It looked exactly like an oasis. He was sure he could make out the tops of trees against the sky. It even seemed to him that he could see birds flying above it.

"Those are probably the herons and the flamingos," he said to himself, and in another minute he had turned all the way around until he felt the warmth of the sun falling on his tail. "Mohammed's son certainly didn't know what he was talking about," said the youngest camel with a snort of laughter. "The oasis is right over there and not in the direction of the sun at all."

He knew he was absolutely right, and he began congratulating himself on his quick eyes and wits. Most young camels would have gone right on running hard toward the sun and never noticed what fools they were making of themselves, he thought, while he had been clever enough to perceive that even the son of the great Prophet of Islam could be wrong.

But before he had gone very far, a flock of herons came flying across the heavens toward him, and as they came near, they circled lower. Closer and closer they came as if in wonder at the sight of a baby camel running so fast across the desert. Then the leader of the herons called down to him:

"Where are you going so fast, four-footed child?"

The youngest camel was annoyed at being called a child by birds he had never laid eyes on before, and he tossed his head rather insolently as he answered:

"I'm on my way to the oasis where my mother is stopping with her caravan. If they've started on by the time I get there, I'll run straight on to Asquzand!"

48

"But you've lost your way, little camel!" the herons called down in a great chorus of voices to him. "We're going to the oasis for the night! Turn around and follow us!"

"You must be as blind as bats, old birds!" the little camel cried out impatiently. "I can see the oasis right straight ahead!"

"No, no, you're going in the wrong direction!" the leader of the herons called down to him, and he beckoned with one wing. "You must keep the sun before you! Don't let its warmth fall on your tail!"

The flock of birds swerved over him once more, calling to him to come, and then they flew off, their legs floating on the air behind them, and the youngest camel paid no attention to them at all. Instead, he started running quickly again toward the dark object on the horizon that seemed no nearer than it had been before. He did not know how long he ran, but now the whole world was turning pink with evening, and he was tired. As he stumbled on, a flock of flamingos came winging toward him, their feathers and legs colored like the petals of a rose. When they saw the little camel running so desperately across the wastes of sand, they circled several times above him, and the leader called out:

"Where are you going, little dromedary?"

"Can't you see I'm going to the oasis?" he cried out in irritation.

He was so tired now that he had to stop running while he talked to them. He felt angry with everyone and every-

thing, and he stamped one hoof in the cooling sand.

"But it's not that way, sweet baby!" the flamingos called down as if in one voice to him. "We're going to the oasis for the night! Follow us and you'll be there before the stars come out!"

When they flew off in the direction in which the herons had gone, the little camel stood for a moment watching them go. And then he tossed his head, and spun around with his back to the sun again, and he began to run. But now that he looked at the oasis lying ahead, it seemed to him to be even farther away than before.

"I'm sure I couldn't have made a mistake," he said half-aloud. "I'm sure I couldn't be wrong. The flamingos and herons don't know what they're talking about."

"Why are you so sure?" asked a clear trilling voice very close to his ear. He looked quickly around, and he saw that scores of brightly feathered little birds were flying and darting in the air about his head. The bird who had spoken to him was no bigger than a pear leaf, but its feathers were as bright as a peacock's tail. All the others were exactly like it, and they spun and darted on the air before him, humming and whistling and watching him with sharp, black, friendly eyes.

"Because I haven't made any mistakes yet in my life," the youngest camel answered boldly. "I can't think of a single time so far that I've been wrong."

At this, all the little birds uttered tiny shrieks of laughter, and those who had alighted on his hump, and on the tips of his ears, swayed back and forth and chattered and chirped in an orchestra of sound. He could feel that some of them were perched on his tail, shrieking with laughter as they swung, and he thrashed it angrily from side to side.

"Well, if you know so much about me," he said furiously, "then just tell me when I did something I shouldn't have done! I know I'm a very good singer because my mother always told me I was, and I know I'm a very good poet because my mother—"

"Oh, good heavens!" screamed the dozens and dozens of little birds with a single voice. "Don't you know that mothers—" But they couldn't finish what they wanted to say, for their shrill laughter trilled and whistled on the evening air.

"I don't know what you think is so funny!" cried the youngest camel. "I'm simply telling you the truth!"

"You speaking the truth!" cried the first little bird as she winged and pirouetted before him. "Do you remember the lie you told your mother about the necklace?"

And now either the last crimson rays of the sun or his own conscience turned the little camel's face bright red, and he hung his head between his legs and looked hard at the sand.

"You've always made the mistake of being conceited," one bird's voice sang clearly and sweetly to him.

"And you made the mistake of not doing what Mohammed's son told you to do," whistled another, while still another trilled:

"You were always a coward except when you were with your mother."

"You made the mistake of not listening to the herons," sang the next bird, and one sitting far back on the youngest camel's tail chirped:

"You made the mistake of insulting the flamingos when they tried to help you! Now they're your enemies for life!"

"But I could see the oasis right before me all the time!" the little camel cried out. If he wasn't careful, he knew

54

he was going to cry. He swung around to point out to them the far, waving palms and the birds hovering over the trees against the horizon ahead, and then he stopped short and stared in amazement, for there was nothing to be seen. "But—but—what's happened—but—there was —but—" he stammered, and the scores of bright small birds took wing from his back and his tail and from the crown of his head and the tips of his ears, and paused a moment with a rush of wings above him.

"You saw a mirage, a mirage! You saw a mirage!" they sang.

In another instant the flock of them had risen straight above him and vanished into nothing in the graying sky. And now that the youngest camel found himself alone in the falling night, he sank down upon his knees in despair. He laid his quivering chin on his forelegs, and sobs shook his bowed little shoulders. He was alone, he was lost, with nothing to eat or drink, and which way lay Asquzand he no longer knew.

"Hope, hope, where are you?" he cried out, but he knew that the magic word had no longer the power to bring Mohammed's son to his side. "Oh, why, why did I let the sun fall warm on my tail?" he wept aloud.

V

As the night wore on, the sand under him grew cooler and cooler, but still the youngest camel could not sleep. He thought of everything his mother had ever said to him, and he thought of Mohammed's son, and of the herons, and the flamingos, and the quick-tongued little birds who had swung on his tail.

"Everyone has advice to give," he said to himself a little impatiently. "Even your own mother tells you what to do and what not to do, and what to be and what not to be. Instead of advice, dreams and poetry and music would be a lot more use." He thought of Mohammed's son saying to him that it was important to be humble; and "I would be humble," he said aloud in the silence of the desert, "if I knew what things are really greater than me."

When the sun came up, tired though he was, he

jumped to his feet and began running toward its light. But in a moment he remembered that it was in the afternoon when Mohammed's son said he should run straight in the direction of the sun, and he stopped short.

"Perhaps I should run with the sun behind me now," he said to himself, and he turned around and went running as fast as he could in the opposite direction, and in spite of his hunger and his thirst he felt that everything was going to be all right now. He was rather pleased with himself because he had worked out the movements of the sun without any help from anyone older and wiser, and he did not mind the loneliness and the nothingness of the desert as much as he had the day before.

On he went with eager, flying feet until, after a little, he saw two black shapes on the pure white sand ahead. They seemed to be two enormous birds with their backs turned to him, and as he came nearer he could see their skulls were as bald as ostrich eggs and as red as gaping wounds. He made a half-circle around them, and then he saw they were tearing fiercely with their curved beaks at something they held between them in their bluish claws.

"Vultures!" he thought, and a tremor of fear went through his heart. But he stepped a little closer to them,

and he said: "Please," in a timid voice. Both birds were so startled that they jumped a yard into the air.

"Snakes alive!" cried one as she landed on the sand again.

"I'm sorry I frightened you," said the youngest camel apologetically.

"Can't you see that we don't want to be interrupted?" said the second vulture. "Annie and I came down here to eat this hare in peace and quiet, and we want to be left alone."

"I just wanted to ask if I'm going in the right direction for Asquzand," said the youngest camel.

When he said this, the birds stopped trying to get the remains of the hare away from each other, and they looked at him with the greatest interest.

"Are you lost?" the one called Annie asked rather eagerly.

"I'm afraid I am," said the little camel, "but I think by running ahead of the sun until noon, and then running toward it all afternoon, I'll find my way to the oasis. Yesterday I didn't do that, so nothing turned out right."

"Ah, but yesterday was yesterday, wasn't it, Mabel?" said Annie, and she gave her sister a sly glance. "Today is today, so everything is very different."

"But the sun always follows the same course," said the youngest camel, and both vultures cackled aloud.

"Where in the world did you get that idea?" cried Mabel, and then she turned to the business before her and began slicing the hare's heart into neat, roast-beef-like pieces with her beak.

"The sun hardly ever does the same thing twice, does it, Mabel?" said Annie. "Some days it runs all over the place, getting behind clouds and mountains and doing whatever it likes. Yesterday it was going from north to south, and today, as you can see for yourself, it's going from east to west."

"If you're really lost," said Mabel, swallowing the

hare's tail in one gulp, "you'll come to know us very well indeed in the end."

Annie picked her teeth reflectively with the yellow claw of one foot, and studied the little camel in silence for a moment. Then she said:

"He's small, of course, but rather well covered with meat."

Suddenly the little camel understood exactly what they meant, and he reared up on his hind legs in fright, and spun around, and began to run. He had no idea which way he was going, but he knew he must get out of sight of the two bald sisters as fast as he could. While he ran, he tried making up some rhymed poetry to steady his nerves, but nothing sounded right to him. He wanted to write a letter to his mother in verse, but he couldn't think of a single original or beautiful line.

> *"Dear Mother,"* (he began) *"how in the world am I*
> *going to dance or sing without you?*
> *I miss your hump and your sore hip and*
> *everything about you.*
> *I've made a fool of myself with every bird*
> *that flies,*
> *And Mohammed's son dislikes me, and I've*
> *told you lies."*

"That isn't poetry," he said to himself. "That's just a plain statement of fact. I've lost every gift I ever had."

But he couldn't help adding:

> *"One or two things I've said are true:*
> *Music, Love, and History*
> *Are still the invisible three,*
> *But Love, invisible it's true,*
> *Still has the shape and smell of you."*

By this time he was so weary that he tottered awkwardly from side to side, and if he hadn't slowed down to a walk he would have toppled over in the sand.

"I have no talent as a poet, or as a singer, and now that I am much too weak to carry a load and walk in a caravan with other camels, I am no good for anything on earth," he said, and there seemed no reason why he should not have sunk down in the blistering heat and quietly breathed his last.

But now that the little camel had admitted he no longer thought his own voice was beautiful, and his own poetry the best in the world, and no longer dreamed of a full-length mirror so that he could see how graceful he looked while he danced, he was able to hear other voices which he had never known existed before. The air that passed his ears seemed to have the power of speech, and as he staggered on, he listened.

"There is an oasis in every camel's desert of despair," said one particle of air to him, and another murmured:

"It cannot be far now, little camel, for you have traveled a long way in suffering as well as in distance."

Even the sand under his feet seemed able to speak, for as it ran through his hoofs he heard it whispering:

"The wind is coming, the wind is coming."

All around him in the desert, one grain of sand murmured to another:

"The wind is coming," and others answered: "In a little while we shall have to rise and dance."

Before he had gone much farther, he saw a lilac-colored cloud of wind coming rapidly across the hot blue sky and here and there the sand began to rise in spirals, whirling and turning and swaying in a frantic dance. Ghost-like figures of sand now spun wildly around him, reaching taller and taller above him while the wind screamed:

"Dance, sand dervishes, dance, dance, dance!"

The youngest camel was almost blinded by the veils of sand which were flung across his eyes, and he could see nothing to the east or west, or the north or south, except

the white, spinning webs of sand. The sun seemed to have
been blown from the sky, and the purple of dusk was all
around him, and he did not know which way to turn.

"Close your eyes," whispered one sand dervish to him.

"Close your lips," whispered another whom the wail-
ing wind blew against him, and a third murmured to
him as she spiraled past:

"Do not breathe deeply. Advice can be poetry and
music as well as wisdom. If you listen to us, you will be
saved."

The youngest camel staggered blindly through the

storm, and now there was no longer any division of time, no night or day, or sun or moon, and finally when he thought he could go no farther, the voice of a sand dervish whirled about his head and whispered to him:

"We have led you to the pathway between the winds. Be patient with all that lies ahead. Farewell."

At once the force of the storm grew less, and the screams of the furious wind grew fainter and fainter, and then a perfect calmness fell on the earth, and in another moment the little camel ventured to open his eyes. Then he stood blinking in bewilderment, for his feet were placed on a carpet of fresh green grasses, and a little rivulet ran, chattering, through the rocks beside him. All about were luxuriant fruit trees with their boughs heavy with fruit, and through the thick, dark leaves he could see the sun was rising. This was the oasis, he thought with joy, and if the sun was rising, then it meant that a day and a night had passed since the sandstorm had begun.

When his eyes had grown accustomed to the beauty of the scene around him, he saw that at the edge of the cool, moss-grown wood there stood a silk tent handsome enough to shelter a rajah or a shah. The brocaded tent flaps were caught back with brooches set with shining jewels, and a thin thread of incense smoke rose languidly from it on the clear morning air. But it was the running water that seemed the most beautiful thing of all to the youngest camel, and he fell gratefully on his knees at the stream's brink. But before he had time to touch the water with his lips, a deep, lazy-sounding voice called out to him from inside the tent:

"Not so fast, not so fast, young camel. You have passed through the final night of the ordeal of loneliness, but the third day is just dawning. Twelve hours lie ahead of you before you may eat or drink. The day which is just being born is the Day of Temptation. Some camels consider it the most difficult day of all."

If anyone had said this to the little camel the week be-

fore, he would have gone right ahead and drunk his fill at the brook. Then he would have run to the big trees and started pulling the fruit down from the heavily laden boughs. But so much had happened to him in the past two days that now he rose obediently without so much as wetting his parched lips, and turned respectfully toward the silken tent.

"Well, you've certainly saved yourself a lot of trouble," the voice went on. "If you hadn't taken my advice, you would be right back in the middle of the sandstorm again, and this time the sand dervishes wouldn't have been allowed to get you out."

"I thought the storm was over," said the little camel with some of his old argumentative spirit.

"Oh, the storm never stops," the lazy voice went on. "It's always there, blowing just as hard as when you were in it. We have to keep it going in order to test the endurance of other young camels. It takes a great deal of energy," said the voice, and it sounded now as if the owner of it were stifling a yawn, "but we have no choice."

"Why were the sand dervishes so kind as to help me to get out?" asked the youngest camel.

"Probably because you said right out in the poem you made up yesterday that you'd made a fool of yourself with everybody you met," the sleepy voice answered. "I'm sure they liked that very much. They like courage and intelligence, and most young camels don't show both at the same time. If you manage to get through today without forgetting the things you've learned, you'll be having a nice sea-shell dinner with your mother this evening in Asquzand."

The youngest camel felt a tremor of joy go through him as he heard these words, and he almost jumped straight up in the air with delight. But his knees were so weak under him that he decided not to make any unnecessary movements, and instead he called out in a happy voice:

"Oh, I know I'll get through today all right!"

"You don't know anything about it," said the voice, and this time the little camel was certain that its owner was yawning as he spoke. "Come in and pay homage to me, and I'll explain things to you more fully."

The youngest camel took a few uncertain steps toward the tent, and then he halted in shyness.

"I'm afraid I don't know how to pay homage," he said.

"Oh, just bow down two or three times, and strike your forehead on the floor," said the drowsy voice. "It doesn't really matter what you do as long as you feel humble inside yourself. It's just part of the rigmarole. Some young camels are so arrogant that they absolutely refuse to do it, and then it's really such a bore for everyone. They have to go right back to Annie and Mabel and be torn to pieces for dinner. It's one of the regulations, and there's nothing I can do."

When he heard this, the youngest camel went quickly into the tent, and there he fell down on his knees and struck his forehead three times on the richly carpeted floor. The smell of incense was strong and sweet on the air, and when his eyes had grown accustomed to the dim light inside the tent, he glanced curiously up at the owner of the voice, and he saw it was an enormously fat and incredibly ancient camel with a coat as white as snow.

The great kingly camel was lying on a divan covered with silk cushions of every color of the rainbow, and his hoofs were painted a shining gold. A necklace of opals as big as alligator eggs hung around his neck, and earrings of opals and tiny bright diamonds, like drops of dew, studded his hairy ears. But it was his eyes which held the youngest camel's attention more than anything else. They were almond-shaped, and large, and black, and heavy lids hung over them, like fringed, white velvet curtains drawn over windows darkened by the night. But every time the white velvet curtains seemed about to close over his eyes, the old camel would snap them up again, and then slowly, sleepily, they again began to fall until he jerked them back. This happened several times before he spoke.

"Stand up," he said with a yawn. "You don't have to overdo it. It's just as bad to be too humble as it is to be too self-satisfied." He looked for a long time at the youngest camel, who had now got to his feet, and at last he said: "You wouldn't be bad-looking if you took the trouble to carry yourself better. Why do you hang your head as if you were ashamed of something?"

"I'll try to do better," said the little camel, and he stood up straighter and lifted his head, but his underlip was quivering with fatigue.

"Oh, it doesn't really make any difference," said the white camel in a voice that was even more sleepy than before. "Everyone has different ideas about things. They tell me men try to make their children sit up straight so that they won't have humps on their backs, and of course mother camels make their children hump themselves for fear their backs will turn out straight. It's just a matter of preference. In case you didn't recognize me," he added, "I'm the leader of the caravan of white camels that circles the earth, and everybody worships me."

"But my mother told me the caravan of white camels didn't exist!" said the youngest camel.

"As long as I can keep awake, we exist," said the white leader. "It's only when I fall asleep that we aren't there any more." His white velvet lids sank so low over his eyes that the youngest camel thought he had fallen asleep now, but immediately he jerked them up again and went on talking. "Everything exists, either in the imagination or else really. But now we must be getting started," he said.

"Where are we going?" asked the youngest camel.

"Oh, nowhere in particular," the old camel answered. "We just go around and around and try to make you give in to one temptation after another. You're the only one who gets any fun out of it because it's all new to you. But if you give in to a single temptation, that's the end as far as you're concerned. Then you have to go all the way back to the first night when the camel drivers tied you out in the desert, and once you're out there bound up again, you die of fright."

The old camel gave such a terrific yawn at this that his servants must have thought they were being called, for at the sound of it two sleek white camels with brocaded bands around their shoulders and brows came in through the door of the tent and kneeled before their leader.

"All right, let's get started," said the old camel, and immediately the two servants rose and slipped their shoulder bands under the two ends of the divan and lifted him, cushions and all, and bore him out of the tent into the light of the softly dawning day. "I hate getting up so early," said the old white camel, and the youngest camel, who trotted along beside him, nodded his head. "Why don't you speak frankly to me?" asked the old leader. "You were thinking I wasn't up at all, weren't you? You felt like saying that I was really more down than up, I'm sure."

"Yes," said the little camel, "I was thinking that."

As soon as he had said these words, he saw that a beautiful pure-white camel had appeared and was following closely behind the litter on which the leader stretched at his ease. The new camel's hoofs were of the finest gold and he wore a halter of spun light—moonlight or sunlight, thought the youngest camel, but which it was he could not tell. When the old leader saw the youngest camel staring in admiration at the new arrival, he said:

"That's Fourteen Carat. He's always the first to join the caravan and that means you've passed through one temptation." They were moving out from under the green trees now, and onto the desert sands. "Of course,

you were tempted to lie when I asked you what you were thinking," the old camel said.

"I don't think it would be really a lie if I said it to spare your feelings," said the youngest camel.

"In this game we're playing, feelings are not to be spared," said the old white leader, and he made a great effort not to yawn. "Most young camels do lie when I ask them, and then it's the end of them. They vanish in a puff of smoke. There's nothing worse than a hypocrite, unless it's a peacock without a tail. I once wrote a poem about a hypocrite," said the old camel, and he called out to the litter bearers to halt. Then he stretched out one golden forefoot, and he traced these lines on the sand:

H

   I

       *P*popotamus

         O,

            *C*reature

              *R*are

                *I*ndeed in every feature,

                    *T*ell me why you smile so widely

                        *E*vening, morning, and noon-tidely?

"Do you like that, not counting the spelling?" he asked.

"No," said the youngest camel in a low voice. "Poems ought to answer questions, not ask them."

"Very well," said the old leader; "if that's what you think, you have a perfect right to say it." But as he motioned to the litter bearers to go on again, he seemed somewhat annoyed. "Every time you do the right thing," he said as he sank wearily back on the cushions, "you will notice that another camel joins our caravan."

The little camel turned his head quickly, and, lo! a second camel was already there.

VI

So, hour after hour, as they traveled across the desert, the ordeal of temptation went on. There was the temptation to crunch the sea-shells which were served on a silver platter within an inch of the youngest camel's nose, and the temptation to drink from copper basins which were carried to him filled with sparkling water. But he set his chin firmly and resisted, and each time he did another white camel joined the caravan. Then came the temptation of salt and tobacco, and the little camel looked at them with longing eyes. For a moment he thought it might be much wiser to take them, for his mother had told him since his earliest days that salt and tobacco were the fare of rajahs and pashas and kings, and if a poor camel ever had the luck to get near them, he should eat them up as quickly as he could.

"This isn't really a meal," said the white leader, who

had already begun to nibble at the delicacies on the enameled plate. "It couldn't possibly do you any harm to try just a little."

"I want to try a little," said the youngest camel, and he was very tired. "But first I'd like to ask you one question because I don't really understand what I'm supposed to learn in the end. Do I have to keep on refusing things for the rest of my life?"

"Oh, no," said the old camel in a sleepy voice. "You're supposed to be acquiring wisdom, and when you have you'll know at once what to take and what to leave alone. Some people recommend eating tobacco to become wise overnight, and others say there's nothing like salt to sharpen the wits."

"And when I've acquired wisdom," asked the youngest camel, "will I still be able to write poetry?"

The white leader chewed on a bit of tobacco as he looked at the little camel for a long moment from under his fringed velvet lids, and then he said:

"That's one of the secrets of life, little camel. I see you are already beginning to be wise. I wonder if you could make up a poem right now that doesn't ask questions but answers them. Please have a try."

So the youngest camel began to recite in a sad and hesitant voice:

> "*I want to be different from what I am*
> *(But not too different). I would like to*
>   *be handsomer,*
> *Braver, and wiser (but not too wise).*
> *I have a musical ear, and a poet's tongue,*
> *And a voice for all the songs to be sung,*
> *But whenever I think of my mother something*
>   *happens to my eyes.*"

"That doesn't answer any questions," said the old camel somewhat critically, and he offered the plate of tobacco and salt to the little camel again.

"I don't think I will after all, but thank you just the same," said the youngest camel, holding back his tears. He knew that the lump in his throat would keep him from swallowing anything, and no sooner had he spoken than another golden-hoofed camel joined the caravan.

And now the old white leader did a thing so natural and simple that there seemed no reason to believe it was a temptation at all. He reached indolently up from his litter as they jogged along, and he drew down the weather to show the youngest camel that it actually was a fan with two sides to it. One side was good weather, and the other was bad, and the old camel suggested that the little camel accept it as a gift. "Think how useful it would be to your mother," said the old white leader, spreading it open. "You could take it to her as a present this evening, and from then on she could always have exactly the kind of weather she wanted."

"But my mother told me once that she doesn't believe the weather is a fan," said the youngest camel.

"It's part of your duty as a son to widen your mother's horizon for her," the old camel said a little sharply. "If you took her this fan, she wouldn't have to get drenched by storms any more or covered with snow on the steppes during the bad season. I can't imagine why you hesitate like this."

"Just because I want it so badly," said the little camel, and suddenly the tears ran down his face.

"Now, stop crying and come over here and take it," said the old camel in a gentler voice. The youngest camel took a step toward him, and then he halted.

"If I had the fan, then I would be Mohammed," he

said, "because the weather belongs to him. And I know I am not Mohammed."

"My child, you are growing very wise," said the old leader with a sigh, and immediately the fan disappeared, and another white camel took its place in the caravan.

Temptation after temptation followed this, and the little camel resisted them all, and then, just as the sun was sinking beyond the horizon and the little camel believed he had come to the end of his strength at last, he saw something so marvelous just ahead that he thought he must be dreaming. Yes, it was. No, it couldn't possibly be. But still it *was*. Yes, surely, it was. The more he looked, the more convinced he became, and suddenly he jumped straight up into the air.

"My mother! I can see my mother over there!" he cried out, and the old white camel lifted himself lazily on one elbow to see.

"Well, I must say it rather looks like her," he said, stifling a yawn. "I wonder what she's doing, wandering about like that alone." He sank back on his cushions again and closed his eyes. "Perhaps she's strayed from her caravan and is wandering around in despair," he said.

"Perhaps she's looking for me!" cried the little camel,

but the old leader only yawned again. She was jogging along not very far ahead of them with her moth-eaten tail hanging down behind, and the youngest camel cried out in joy: "It is my mother! I know it's my mother!"

"No one ever said it wasn't," said the old camel, and this time it really sounded as if he were falling asleep. "But you can't possibly be sure at this distance whether it's your mother or just a striking likeness."

"But I couldn't mistake my own mother, could I?" asked the youngest camel. "I know the way her elbows look from the back, and the way her hump humps—"

"There's only one way to find out for certain," said the old white leader. "You'd better skip along and catch up with her."

"Oh, would you excuse me for a moment while I do?" asked the little camel, so excited that he could scarcely wait.

The old leader gave a terrific yawn at this and stretched himself out as if for a long sleep. Without waiting another moment, the youngest camel started off at a gallop across the hot stretches of sand toward where she ambled along. But he was so tired by now that he stumbled over his own feet, and he found he was gasping and choking for breath, and he seemed to be getting no nearer to her.

"Mother!" he cried out. "Mother! Wait! I'm coming!"

But just then a sudden burst of bright-feathered little birds descended between them and set about his eyes and ears like a swarm of bees. They were all chattering wildly, and he could no longer see beyond them because of the fluttering of their wings.

"Oh, let me go! Please, let me go!" he pleaded, but the sound of his voice was drowned out by the whistling and scolding of the dozens and dozens of little birds. Some had settled on his hump, and some on his head, while others flew furiously back and forth before his eyes. He spun around, but they were everywhere, increasing in numbers and fury, chattering, warbling, and swinging like sharp-clawed monkeys on his tail. "Let me go!" he cried in despair to them, and one single brilliant bird poised before him on the air for a moment, and said:

"Listen to us once again, little camel. You have lost a great deal of your conceit since we last met, and you have almost entirely ceased to lie."

"Yes, yes, yes!" trilled all the birds in chorus.

"You are much braver now," the single bird's voice went on. "You have become much humbler than you ever were before."

"Yes, yes, yes!" cried the shrill little voices again.

"So now, go back!" warbled the bird who winged before him on the air. "Go back, go back before the white leader opens his eyes!"

"Yes, yes, yes!" cried all the little birds in the shrillest chorus he had ever heard, and suddenly the youngest camel's knees began to shake under him. Was it possible that this was just one more temptation that had been put to him?

"But I'm sure—I'm absolutely certain—I know I saw my mother," he protested, and as he said this all the birds rose up from his back and from his head and from his tail, and they filled the air again with the rushing of their wings.

"Look, four-footed child!" sang the single bird's voice to him. "Look ahead and look well at her. She's nothing. She's just a reflection on the mists of evening. Can't you see she's a mirage like the oasis you followed?"

"Yes, a mirage, a mirage!" trilled the hundreds of birds around him.

The youngest camel turned in his track, with just enough breath left to call out his thanks to the little birds, and he made his way back to the caravan as quickly as he could. His knees were still shaking under him when he reached the litter, and from there he saw the flock of tiny bright birds disappear like a sunset cloud into the sky.

"So here you are after all!" said the old white camel as he sat up with a start.

"Yes," said the little camel in a low voice. He was so tired that he could scarcely stand.

And now that the day was nearly done, the old camel reached out and plucked the setting sun out of the sky, and he cut it in pieces on a great salver which the camel servants held before him.

"You see, it's a pineapple with the skin taken off. That's all the sun is," said the old white camel. "It has a wonderful flavor, much nicer than anything you've ever tasted before."

"It looks awfully good," said the youngest camel, and he felt his mouth watering.

"Well, there's no earthly reason why you shouldn't have a piece. I'm going to," said the old camel, and he indolently chose the biggest, juiciest bit on the plate and put it in his mouth. The little camel stood watching him enviously as he chewed, and licked his own parched lips.

"My mother told me it wasn't true about the sun being a pineapple," the little camel said.

"Oh, mothers have so much on their minds that sometimes they can't remember what things are real and what things aren't," said the old camel while the juices dribbled down his chin. "If you just take a piece you'll see it's true enough."

He selected another ripe golden piece and conveyed it lazily to his lips, and the little camel turned his head away. For a moment it seemed to him that he would refuse just because refusing everything, whether it made any sense or not, seemed the thing he was supposed to do. And then, suddenly, everything became clearer to him than it had ever been before.

"I want the weather to be the weather, and the sun to be the sun," he said, and he looked bravely at the old white leader. "I don't want to have one for a fan and eat the other like a pineapple. I like them better the way they are."

And at once in the blue dusk of the early evening a thousand torches suddenly sprang alight the whole length of the magic caravan. The youngest camel could see the endless line of camels girdling the earth with the flaming torches carried on their heads, and their gold hoofs shining wondrously as they followed across the slipping sands.

"It's rather effective, isn't it?" said the old white leader, looking quite pleased at the whole display. There were four tall torches lit about him now, two at his head and two at his feet, and the diamonds in his ornaments glittered in their light. "This is the part I like best because it's so near the end, and then I can go to sleep," he said.

He felt under his cushions for a moment, and drew forth a beautiful necklace, and as the light of the torches shone on it the youngest camel recognized it at once. The beads of it were of different colors, and his heart leapt with delight when he saw the bright blue one, and the clear green one, and the moonstone, and the diamond. He could even make out the tiny lettering which was carved in the center of each one.

"These are magic beads," the old camel said, holding them up so that the jewels took the brilliance of the torch-light. "They're the most valuable possession anyone could possibly have because they're practically impossible."

"Oh, yes, I know, I know!" cried the youngest camel.

"How could you know?" asked the white leader.

"Because I think I invented them," said the little camel eagerly, and then he couldn't help saying: "Have you ever tried them? Do they work?"

"Of course they work," said the old camel.

"Well, then, excuse me," said the youngest camel, "but

why don't you live in a green valley forever, the way the jade bead says you can?"

"Because I prefer to travel on a litter and see the world," said the white leader. "I'd be very bored lying in a valley without any change of scenery, year in, year out."

"If you'll excuse me again," said the youngest camel, "and I hope you won't think I'm rude—why don't you press the sapphire against your forehead for an instant and have all your years drop away from you like the petals from a flower?"

"You mean turn myself young again?" asked the big white camel in amazement. "Do you really imagine I'd like to start way back at the beginning again and do all the silly things I did over, and not have people in every country in the world paying me homage and not be the leader of the caravan of white camels any more?" He sank back on his pillows again and gave a weary sigh. "I never heard anything quite so silly in all my life," he murmured, and this time he did not try to hide his yawn.

The youngest camel stood looking with longing eyes at the necklace and thinking of the words that were written in each bead. In the topaz would be inscribed: "I am a silk tent to protect you from sandstorms and from winter and from the midday sun," and in the ruby there would be: "I am blood to flow in your veins and the veins of those you love. Thus you may live forever," and in the ivory bead would be the poem about oysters and clams and periwinkles rising from the sea.

"But then I should think if you have no use for the necklace you wouldn't mind giving it away, or at least lending it to others sometimes," said the little camel.

"Naturally, as long as I have everything I want, I haven't the slightest use for it," said the old white camel, "but so many people wanting it makes it very valuable indeed. That's why it's kept till the very end like this. Now that you've resisted all the temptations, you're allowed to have a choice."

He held the necklace up in the torchlight again, and the little camel fell on one knee.

"Do you mean—do you mean I can choose—do you mean I—" he stammered.

"Now, don't get excited," said the old leader. "This is the final test, remember. You are allowed to choose between this string of magic beads and—" He made a gesture toward a great bulging sack which the camel servants had just placed on the sand beside his litter. "And this bag," he said. "I do hope you're not going to make a mistake at the last minute."

"What's in the bag?" asked the little camel in a cautious voice, and the old leader answered:

"Ashes. Nothing but ashes."

"But I can't see that there's any choice at all!" the little camel cried out. "Of course, I'll take the—"

"Now, don't be in too much of a hurry to make up your mind," said the old white camel. "Remember greediness never got anybody anywhere at all, and things are rarely what they seem. Don't forget that appearances are frequently deceiving, and keep in mind that there are always a lot of wolves in sheep's clothing about, even right here on the desert." The young camel stood reflecting deeply while the old white leader went on: "I'm sure you don't want to act like an uneducated little pig just when everything seems to be turning out rather well for you."

"No," said the little camel gravely, "but I want the necklace. I don't want the sack of ashes. I want the necklace more than anything else in the world."

"Of course you do," said the old camel, and in spite of the fact that he was very much interested in the conversation, his lids kept slipping down over his eyes. "Naturally, we all want what isn't good for us, but that doesn't mean you're going to be a silly, grasping little camel and—"

"Please," said the youngest camel in a firm voice. "I choose the necklace. That's what I want."

"Well, I must say that's very unkind of you," said the old white leader, and he tossed it around the little camel's neck with rather a nasty jerk. "No young camel ever chose the necklace before. Everyone's always chosen the bag of ashes."

The youngest camel felt his heart singing so loudly in his breast that it seemed to him the entire caravan could hear it, and poems were writing themselves with twice the speed of light across his mind. He thanked the old leader for his gift, and he stepped back from the litter, and as he began his song, his voice rang out with a strength that it had never had before.

"Come, Night, and wrap me in your dark blue
cloak!" he sang.
"Your stars are sands of higher deserts. I
am not afraid!"

And then he broke off suddenly, for he remembered what he had said to the old camel about wanting things to be exactly as they were.

"The night is not a dark blue cloak," he said to himself, and it seemed of the greatest importance to him that he had found this out; "and the stars are certainly not grains of sand. They are stars!"

So he sang instead:

> "Oh, I am as humble as humble pie (since an
>   hour or two),
> And I heed the advice of birds that fly
>   (flamingos, herons, and vultures, too);
> For I've learned what is really greater than I:
> Mohammed's son, and the planets that rise, and
>   the tears I saw in my mother's eyes.
> I've become the humblest camel alive (but I'm
>   not too humble),
> And I'm the youngest camel I know who is not
>   afraid of the dark."

He paused, then, to find a word that would rhyme with "dark," and as he repeated "bark," and "hark," and "lark," he saw that the fringed velvet lids were slowly dropping over the old white camel's eyes. And now it was just as he had told the little camel at the beginning: the moment he slept the caravan of camels no longer existed, and suddenly the litter was gone, and the white leader with it, and the little camel was left standing there alone on the wide stretches of sand. Immediately, he turned the necklace of shining jewels around and around on his neck, passing the emerald that would be the green vale for his mother to rest in, and the sapphire that would make the years drop away from her like the petals of a flower, letting all the beads slip by, one by one, until he came to the one that was shaped like a heart and as red as a cherry, and he read out loud the inscription which was written inside it:

> *"Oh, heart, that does all children understand,*
> *Bear me this summer night to Asquzand!"*

And in the flick of a tail he was lifted up from the desert sands and taken there just as the caravan kneeled down to rest.